To James

Henry Holt and Company
Publishers since 1866
175 Fifth Avenue New York, New York 10010
mackids.com

Henry Holt® is a registered trademark of Macmillan Publishing Group, LLC.
Copyright © 2017 by Adam Auerbach

Library of Congress Cataloging-in-Publication Data is available.
ISBN 978-1-62779-600-2

Our books may be purchased in bulk for promotional, educational, or business use. Please contact your
local bookseller or the Macmillan Corporate and Premium Sales Department at (800) 221-7945 ext. 5442
or by e-mail at MacmillanSpecialMarkets@macmillan.com.

First Edition—2017 / Designed by Eileen Savage
The artist used pen and ink, watercolor, and digital color to create the illustrations for this book.
Printed in China by Toppan Leefung Printing Ltd., Dongguan City, Guangdong Province
10 9 8 7 6 5 4 3 2 1

MONKEY BROTHER

Adam Auerbach

Christy Ottaviano Books

Henry Holt and Company • New York

My little brother is a monkey.

I'm not kidding.

He really is.

Having a little monkey
for a brother isn't easy.

I never get a
minute to myself.

He follows me
everywhere.

I mean **everywhere**.

The way he treats my dog, Gerald, is awful.

Just **awful**.

He's always making messes.

Always . . .

We take him
to the park to
wear him out.

But he **just**

keeps

going.

Sometimes this little friend of his comes over.

One monkey is bad enough.
Two of them

can really

make you

crazy.

I thought it couldn't
get any worse . . .

... until the birthday party happened.

And if that's not
bad enough, he's
always copying me.

I mean **always**.

Well . . .

. . . **almost** always.

Once in a while, the little guy surprises me.

And I remember that my little brother can be pretty fun sometimes

and even kind of sweet.

Having a monkey brother can come in handy.

He's especially great
at tickle wars.

To tell you the truth,
my brother and I have
been getting along pretty
well lately.

Now, my baby sister—
well that's a different story.